To:

From:

ALWAYS SO GRUMPY

WORDS BY ERIN GUENDELSBERGER
PICTURES BY ANDOTWIN

sourcebooks
wonderland

I am grumpy. I am crabby.

I am *not* having a good day.

See these spines? They're not just for looks.

They're prickly, so watch out!

You want to try to cheer me up? You could try telling a funny joke or making a silly noise. It's not going to work, but go ahead. I'll wait while you try your best one.

Okay, that was pretty funny.

But I am always so grumpy.

See? Here is my grumpy face.

What's next? Are you going to tickle me? Try it. It won't make any difference.

You can tickle my belly. Under my arm.
Under my chin. Behind my ear.
I won't smile. I won't laugh.
I. Am. Always. So. GRUMPY!

I bet you think I need a nap to feel better.
You think I should get into that hammock?
I'll get in—you can even rock me!
But it isn't going to help.
And I'm NOT tired!

Hold on a second.

Maybe try rocking me a little bit more.

Ouch! You rocked me too hard!
Now I'm sore AND grumpy.
And look at this mess you've made!
You're going to have to shake the book to get
everything back in order.

It may be cleaner now,
but I am still done, done, DONE.
I'm going to build a fence so I can be by myself.

It's not a big fence, but it will do
for now. And don't try knocking on it,
because I won't come out! I'm still grumpy.

Hey! You made my fence fall down!

That's it! You leave me no choice.

You might as well put the book down and walk away.
I'm going to stay in this ball until you leave me alone.

Wait! Are you really going away?

Couldn't you stay a little bit longer?

The truth is, I woke up this morning
feeling cranky and kind of gloomy.
Maybe you could give me a hug?
And say…"I love you"?

Wow! That's much better.

I guess I'm not *always* so grumpy.

Thanks for sticking with me, even when I wasn't very much fun to be around. You're a good friend.

Psst. I love you too!

For Zooey and Ada, whom I love
happy, grumpy, and everywhere in between.

—EG

For everyone who needs a big hug.

—AT

Published by Sourcebooks Wonderland, an imprint of Sourcebooks Kids
P.O. Box 4410, Naperville, Illinois 60567-4410
(630) 961-3900
sourcebookskids.com

Library of Congress Cataloging-in-Publication Data is on file with the publisher.

Source of Production: PrintPlus, Shenzhen, Guangdong Province, China
Date of Production: May 2020
Run Number: 5018354

Printed and bound in China.
PP 10 9 8 7 6 5 4 3 2 1